Postcards from • Postales desde

WASHINGTON D.C.

Traveling with Anna • De viaje con Ana

★ Laura Crawford ★

To Madilynn, Lauren and Jackson—
the best nieces and nephew in the world

Text Copyright © 2008 Laura Crawford
Illustration and Translation Copyright © 2008 Raven Tree Press

Crawford, Laura.
Illustrations by Bonnie Adamson
Book Design by Amanda Chavez

Postcards from Washington, D.C. / written by Laura Crawford ; translated by Eida de la Vega = Postales desde Washington, D.C. / escrito por Laura Crawford ; traducción al español de Eida de la Vega — 1st ed. — McHenry, IL : Raven Tree Press, 2008.
     p. ; cm

Text in English and Spanish.

Summary: Join Anna in her travel adventures to the capital of the United States, New York City. Child writes postcards home to friends with facts about historical and tourist sites in this location included.

ISBN: 978–0–9795477–0–6 hardcover
ISBN: 978–0–9795477–1–3 paperback

1. People &Places/United States — Juvenile fiction. 2.Biographical/United States — Juvenile fiction.   3. People & Places/United States — Juvenile non fiction.
4. Bilingual books — English and Spanish. 5. [Spanish language materials—books.]
I. Title II. Title Postales desde Washington, D.C.

Library of Congress Control Number: 2007939495

Printed in Taiwan
10 9 8 7 6 5 4 3 2 1
First Edition

Raven Tree Press
A Division of Delta Publishing Company
www.raventreepress.com

Hi! My name is Anna. I'm going on vacation with my parents to Washington, D.C. I studied our capital in school this year. I loved learning about the presidents in social studies class. I told my mom that I want to be the first woman president! Dad says I can send postcards to my friends and family every day. I'm so excited!

¡Hola! Me llamo Anna. Voy de vacaciones a Washington, D.C., con mis padres. Este año, en la escuela, estudié nuestra capital. Me encanta aprender sobre los presidentes en la clase de estudios sociales. Le dije a mi mamá que quiero ser la primera mujer presidenta. Papá me dijo que puedo enviar postales a mis amigos y a mi familia todos los días. ¡Estoy tan contenta!

Dear Grandma and Grandpa,

I'm having a great time! My first airplane ride was awesome. Did you know the capital city was named after George Washington? The D.C. stands for District of Columbia. I learned that Washington, D.C. isn't in a state, instead it is a district. They have a mayor and government, but Congress has the most authority here. See you when I get home!

Cariños, Anna

★ George Washington was the first president of the United States.

★ The capital city has millions of visitors each year.

★ There are 3 branches of the government in the United States: executive, legislative and judicial.

Washington, D.C.

★ George Washington fue el primer presidente de los Estados Unidos.

★ La capital recibe a millones de visitantes cada año.

★ El gobierno de los Estados Unidos está dividido en tres ramas: la ejecutiva, la legislativa y la judicial.

The White House

★ The address of the White House is 1600 Pennsylvania Avenue.

★ It has 412 doors, 147 windows and 28 fireplaces.

★ President Benjamin Harrison kept a pet goat at the White House.

Dear María,

Today we went to the White House. I looked for the president, but he was busy working with other world leaders. The White House has 132 rooms; there are 3 elevators, a movie theater and over 30 bathrooms. The East Room is so gigantic that the Roosevelt children roller-skated in it. That would be fun.

I miss you! Anna

★ La dirección de la Casa Blanca es 1600 Pennsylvania Avenue.

★ Tiene 412 puertas, 147 ventanas y 28 chimeneas.

★ El presidente Benjamin Harrison tuvo una cabra de mascota en la Casa Blanca.

Hi Jackson,

Today we went to the National Mall. The first thing we saw was the Washington Monument. It looks like a huge, white, 555-foot pencil sticking out of the ground. The marble is 2 different shades of white because it came from 2 different places. We went to the top in an elevator and saw the whole city. It was so windy that it made the building move a little. It was amazing.

Bye for now, Anna ♡

★ 50 American flags are at the base — 1 for each state.

★ It's the highest stone structure in the world.

★ There are 897 steps inside.

★ En la base, hay cincuenta banderas de los Estados Unidos, una por cada estado.

★ Es la estructura de piedra más alta del mundo.

★ En su interior hay 897 escalones.

Washington Monument

9

IN THIS TEMPLE
AS IN THE HEARTS OF THE PEOPLE
FOR WHOM HE SAVED THE UNION
THE MEMORY OF ABRAHAM LINCOLN
IS ENSHRINED FOREVER

Lincoln Memorial

★ Lincoln's nickname was Honest Abe.

★ Lincoln lived in a log cabin when growing up.

★ He had very little formal schooling.

Hola Abuela,

Mom and Dad took me to see the Lincoln Memorial. Abraham Lincoln was the president who freed the slaves during the Civil War. The statue of Lincoln is 19 feet tall. One hand is a fist to show that he was powerful. His other hand is open to show that he was also gentle. I wanted to climb on his lap, but Mom said no.

Adiós, Anna ♡

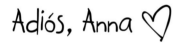

★ El apodo de Lincoln era Abe, el honesto.
★ De niño, Lincoln vivió en una cabaña de troncos.
★ Tuvo muy poca formación escolar.

Dear Aunt Linda and Uncle Jason,

Today we saw the Reflecting Pool. I wanted to go swimming, but Dad said it's not that kind of pool. Martin Luther King Jr. delivered his "I Have a Dream" speech here. I can't wait to tell my teacher I stood right where he spoke!

Hasta pronto, Anna ♡

★ Almost 200,000 people listened to the "I Have a Dream" speech.

★ He was the youngest man to win the Nobel Peace Prize.

★ He was killed on April 4, 1968.

★ Casi 200,000 personas escucharon el discurso "Tengo un sueño".

★ Él ha sido la persona más joven en recibir el Premio Nobel de la Paz.

★ Lo asesinaron el 4 de abril de 1968.

Reflecting Pool

13

The Capitol

★ The Capitol's dome weighs almost 9 million pounds.

★ Underground tunnels connect the Capitol and Congressional buildings.

★ The British set the Capitol Building on fire in the War of 1812.

Hi Paula,

It rained today, so we went to the Capitol. It has 540 rooms! Congress meets there to make our laws. Congress is made up of the Senate and the House of Representatives. I'm going to be a congresswoman when I grow up. I'd like to make the rules and be the boss.

Later, Anna ♡

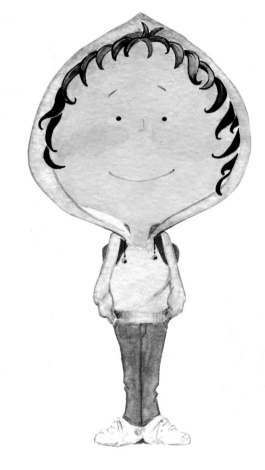

★ La cúpula del Capitolio pesa casi 9 millones de libras.

★ Hay túneles subterráneos que comunican al Capitolio con el Congreso.

★ Los ingleses le prendieron fuego al Capitolio durante la Guerra de 1812.

Hola Bonita,

Today we toured the biggest library in the whole world — the Library of Congress. I wanted to use my library card, but Mom says nothing can be checked out. It has over 100 million books, pictures and other historical stuff. At the National Archives, I saw part of the Declaration of Independence. John Hancock's signature is the biggest. See mine...

Anna

★ The Library of Congress has a bible from 1455.

★ There is a collection of over 2,000 baseball cards from the 1800s and 1900s.

★ 56 men signed the Declaration of Independence.

Library of Congress

★ La Biblioteca del Congreso tiene una Biblia de 1455.

★ Hay una colección de más de 2,000 tarjetas de béisbol de los siglos XIX y XX.

★ 56 hombres firmaron la Declaración de Independencia.

Vietnam Veterns Memorial

★ The architect was a college student.

★ It took 3½ years to build the memorial.

★ The Wall is made of shiny, polished black granite.

Hello Aunt Ceil,

Today we went to the Vietnam Veterans Memorial. There are over 58,000 names carved in the stone. It was very quiet because everyone was remembering the soldiers. We found Uncle Jim's name and I put flowers there. You would be so proud.

Thinking of you, Anna ♡

★ La arquitecta fue una estudiante universitaria.

★ Demoró tres años y medio construir el monumento.

★ Los muros del monumento están hechos de granito negro pulido.

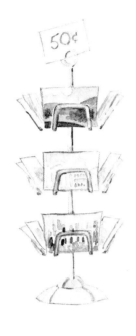

Dear Mrs. Ramírez and class,

Today we visited the Jefferson Memorial. Thomas Jefferson wrote the Declaration of Independence to gain freedom from England. He also was a scientist and inventor. I'm not surprised he has a monument named after him!

See you soon, Anna ♡

★ Thomas Jefferson was our third president.
★ Jefferson spoke 5 languages.
★ He was a lawyer, an author, and a musician.

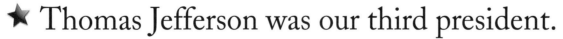

★ Thomas Jefferson fue nuestro tercer presidente.
★ Jefferson hablaba cinco idiomas.
★ Era abogado, escritor y músico.

Jefferson Memorial

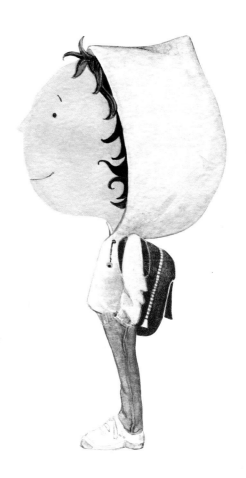

21

Smithsonian Museum of Natural History

★ The Smithsonian Museum has 19 museums and a zoo.

★ Some of the museums are located in New York.

★ The National Museum of Natural History has fossils that are 3.5 million years old.

Hi MaryAnn,

Today we went to one of the Smithsonian Museums. Dad liked the Wright brothers' old wooden plane at the Air and Space Museum. My favorite thing was the spacecraft that went to the moon. I touched a real moon rock. Mom's favorite was the Spirit of St. Louis — the airplane that Charles Lindbergh flew across the Atlantic. We'll be flying home soon.

Love ya, Anna ♡

★ El Museo Smithsonian comprende 19 museos y un zoológico.

★ Algunos de los museos están en Nueva York.

★ El Museo Nacional de Historia Natural tiene fósiles de hace 3.5 millones de años.

¿Qué pasa, Miguel?
Today we visited the coolest place ever — the Federal Bureau of Investigation — FBI for short. The Special Agents that work there are like police officers who solve big crimes and mysteries. I'm going to be an FBI agent someday. I won't be able to tell you about it though, because I'll be undercover!

Your Secret Agent, Anna ♡

★ The FBI is responsible for the "Most Wanted" list of criminals.

★ The FBI started in 1908 with 10 Special Agents — today there are over 11,000.

★ Special Agents graduate from college and train for 16 weeks with the FBI.

Federal Bureau of Investigation

★ El FBI es quien publica la lista de los criminales más buscados.

★ El FBI comenzó en 1908 con 10 agentes especiales. Hoy tiene más de 11,000.

★ Los agentes especiales se gradúan de la universidad y entrenan 16 semanas en el FBI.

Arlington National Cemetery

★ The Tomb of the Unknown Soldier is located here.

★ The unidentified remains of soldiers from World War I were buried here in 1921.

★ Unidentified veterans from World War II and the Korean War were buried here later.

Dear Paul,

Today we went to Arlington National Cemetery. Dad said we should be respectful and quiet to honor the dead. The eternal flame burns near the grave of President John F. Kennedy and his family. A guard marched 21 steps, clicked his heels, faced the tomb, waited 21 seconds, and marched back. All presidents are honored with a 21 gun salute.

Love always, Anna ♡

★ Aquí está la tumba del soldado desconocido.

★ Los restos no identificados de soldados de la I Guerra Mundial se enterraron aquí en 1921.

★ Más tarde, los restos no identificados de soldados de la II Guerra Mundial y de la Guerra de Corea se enterraron aquí.

Hi Alberto,

Today we went to Union Station. Over 25 million people come through here each year. Some were taking the train to work; others were tourists like us. It's not just a train station. There are over 130 places to shop and eat. It even has movie theaters. Mom says she could live here!

Hasta luego, Anna ♡

★ The original Union Station was built in 1908.
★ At that time, it was the largest train station in the world.
★ It cost 160 million dollars to remodel Union Station.

Union Station

★ La *Union Station* original se construyó en 1908.

★ En esa época era la estación de trenes más grande del mundo.

★ Costó $160 millones remodelar *Union Station*.

Bureau of Engraving

★ The Bureau prints 66 billion dollars a year.

★ Special ink is used to stop criminals from making their own money.

★ The Bureau redesigns currency every 7 to 10 years, except for the $1 and $2 bills.

Dear Señor Martínez,

Today I learned about one of my favorite things in the whole world — money! The Bureau of Engraving and Printing is one of the places that prints United States currency. Money isn't made out of paper. It is really linen and cotton. That's why it doesn't get ruined in the washing machine! Mom bought me a page of dollar bills as a souvenir.

Sinceramente, Anna

★ Esta oficina imprime 66 mil millones de billetes de a dólar al año.

★ Se usa una tinta especial para evitar que los falsificadores fabriquen su propio dinero.

★ La oficina rediseña el dinero cada 7 a 10 años, excepto los billetes de $1 y $2.

I loved visiting washington D.C. I liked seeing where the president lives and works! I can't wait to go back!

★ ★ ★

Me encantó visitar Washington, D.C. Me gustó ver dónde vive y trabaja el presidente. ¡Estoy impaciente por volver!